China is a vast country, rich in history and tradition.
Despite its relative old age, however, China has
experienced the growth pains of a new nation ever since it
became a communist country in 1949; not only has China
survived, but her people work hard, and try to find the Chinese
way of living in a modern world.
Foreign missionaries had been living in China for
hundreds of years before the 1950's, when most were
asked to leave.
After they were gone, the leadership of the Christian
church fell into the hands of Chinese Christians. Since that
time, Christians in China have spread the word, discipled
one another, and at times endured persecution.
Their dedication and courage have cultivated the seeds
planted by missionaries years before. The fruit of their
efforts can be seen in this decade, when the Chinese
church has become one of the fastest-growing group of
believers in the world.
This book is dedicated to the Christians of China, who
have endured, and to the mystery of China, which
continues to make it one of the most fascinating countries
in the world.

LI HUA
THE GIRL WHO FOUND ACCEPTANCE
by Douglas Blackwood
Photos by Douglas Blackwood
© Copyright 1987 by Scandinavia
Publishing House, Nørregade 32, DK-1165 Copenhagen K.
English-language edition first published 1988
through special arrangement with Scandinavia
jointly by Wm.B. Eerdmans Publishing Co.,
255 Jefferson Ave. S.E. Grand Rapids, Michigan 49503

Printed in Hong Kong

ISBN 0-8028-5024-3

LI HUA
The Girl Who Found Acceptance

Douglas Blackwood

Photos by Douglas Blackwood

William B. Eerdmans Publishing Company
Grand Rapids, Michigan

"Beautiful Flower." That is what Li Hua's name meant. In China, a name has always been very important. Li Hua should have been proud of her name, a pretty little girl's name. But Li Hua wished she were a boy. She wished and wished, and in the end her wish, in one way, came true. But it did not happen as she expected. Instead something else happened, something much more special than what she ever dreamed could happen.

One day Li Hua went to the open market with her mother. The market was in a town near her little village, in the south of China. Many people came from all over to sell spinach, spices, sugar cane, and seeds. Chickens and ducks poked their heads out of cane baskets. They would soon be sold.

There was a lot of shouting. Li Hua watched a woman argue to get a cheaper price. "**Tai gui**! Too dear!" she shouted.

The seller yelled back, "**Bu, pian ye**! No, cheap!" He placed a duck on a hand-scale and said, "Look! Very big! Not skinny!" Li Hua thought the duck looked very sad, hanging upside-down. She was too busy watching the duck to notice her mother was no longer by her side. The duck's legs were tied and the buyer carried it off, strapped to the handlebars of her bicycle.

Li Hua looked around. Where was Mother? She had lost Mother! There were so many people. She had to push her way between their legs. Quickly! Quickly!

"Oh no! I'll never find Mama." She was very worried. She did not see anyone she knew. Instead, there were old, wrinkled faces, poor, lean faces, laughing toothy grins, and dirty, begging hands. In every direction there was a sea of people squatting, standing, hunched over, pushing and pulling carts, and carrying heavy buckets dangling from bamboo poles balanced over their shoulders.

Li Hua ran up and down the market rows. She could not find Mother anywhere.

Suddenly, Li Hua heard a lot of loud noises. Bang...bang, bang...bang! The sound grew louder and louder until Li Hua had to put her hands over her ears.

There, coming up the street, was a sort of parade of people. In front, several men lit bunches of firecrackers. Behind them walked people carrying flags. But they did not look happy.

Li Hua stopped to watch. What could it all be for? Then she saw people walking behind the flags. They were bent over and walking backwards. They moaned and groaned and looked so sad that other people had to hold them up.

One woman ran away from the people who had been trying to hold her up. She ran farther down the street, then fell onto the ground, crying. The men around her carried a large coffin covered with brightly-colored paper flowers.

"Mama! Mama!" the woman cried.

Then Li Hua knew. The parade was a funeral, and this woman's mother was dead, in the coffin. The woman who was crying wore a white scarf on her head. In China, white represented sadness and death. Red was the color for happiness. Some Chinese believe in luck and magic. The noisy firecrackers and all the yelling were to frighten off the evil spirits they thought brought bad luck.

Li Hua was a little bit afraid of the idea of evil spirits. "Mama," she cried. "Mama, Mama!" But no one heard her call because all around her people yelled in the funeral procession.

Li Hua wanted to get away from the funeral. She ran back to the market. There were so many people, and it seemed like they were all shouting, trying to sell something. Li Hua looked and looked, but she could not find her mother.

Then, suddenly, Li Hua saw an old man she knew. He was sitting with some other people around a stone table, playing a game called **zhi pai**.

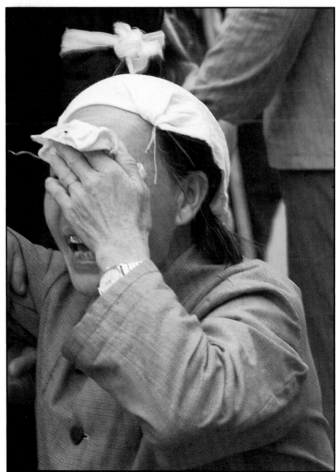

"Bobo," she said. That is what all Chinese children call older men. It meant "Older Uncle." She bowed down to show she respected him. "I am Li Hua, the daughter of Zhang Yong Kang."

The man looked at her with soft, dark eyes. "Yes! I know you now! Where's your family?"

"I don't know. I've lost my mother." Li Hua tried to hold back her tears.

"Don't worry; come with me, my Beautiful Flower. We'll stand on the steps of the People's Hall." The large building, bearing a big "Red Star," the symbol for China, overlooked the whole market. The man's name was Lu Ming De, which meant "Wise and Virtuous." Li Hua felt safe with him.

"Did you know I was a good friend of your great-uncle?" he asked. Li Hua shook her head no. "He was a fine man. Many people respected him because he dared to disagree with China's leaders. These leaders had tried to destroy all the old customs and religions. Many, many good people were killed during that terrible time, called the 'Cultural Revolution.'"

Even though that time had ended just before Li Hua was born, she had never been told about it at home or in school. No one ever talked about it.

"What happened to my great-uncle?" she asked. Bobo Lu made her feel very grown up, talking to her this way.

"Some people took him away. We never saw him again. Bless his name."

Li Hua was just about to ask another question when she saw her mother in the crowd. Quickly, she ran down the steps to catch her. She turned around to look for Bobo Lu, but he was already gone.

At first Mother was very mad at Li Hua for getting lost. Then she just gave her a big hug. Li Hua, though, was still thinking about what Bobo Lu had said. "Mama, why was my great-uncle killed?"

Mother was very surprised. "You should never talk about that time. It will only bring bad luck," she said.

But Mother's answer just made Li Hua want to ask more questions. And why wasn't Bobo Lu afraid of bad luck?

Li Hua and her mother went home by bus. They passed many, many rice paddies and big, high mountains. Hundreds of peaks stood one behind the other as far as Li Hua could see. Everything was so pretty, that it was hard to believe there had ever been a terrible Cultural Revolution and all the killing it caused.

Li Hua's mother had to hurry home to work in the rice paddies. The job of turning the mud over in the flooded paddies with a plow pulled by oxen was done. The rice plants were now growing tall. Mother's back-breaking task was to pull out the rice crops by hand. The whole village came out to help. China grew more rice than any other country. Boiled rice, **fan**, was the main diet of its people.

Li Hua's father fished on the river at night using cormorant birds. The birds could swim very well. They would dive off the boat and catch fish with their beaks. The birds' necks were tied with string so they could not swallow the fish. Li Hua thought it wasn't fair to the birds since they did all the hard work and Father just took the fish out of the birds' mouths. But Father laughed and pointed out it was hard work not to fall off the narrow bamboo raft.

Li Hua's grandmother also lived with them. She had to work too, growing silkworms. Raw silk was obtained from their cocoons. The hungry worms were constantly eating mulberry leaves, and they ate so loudly, that the whole house was filled with the sound of crunching leaves.

Whenever the worms were spinning their cocoons, the whole family had to avoid loud noises and speak in hushed whispers, or the fussy creatures would stop their work. Grandmama explained that was why silk was so expensive. The Chinese discovered silk over three thousand years ago.

Li Hua's family was happy, even though life was hard. It had taken them six months to save enough to buy a radio-cassette recorder. Li Hua remembered when Father had brought it home. The whole village had come around to look at it.

Now there was only one more thing Father wished for, and that was to have a son. A son would mean there would be someone to work for and support the family when Father grew old. A daughter, though, would leave her family when she married. Father talked so often about a son, that Li Hua thought he wished she had been a boy instead of a girl.

Mother, too, hoped to have a son. The mothers in the village who had a boy were very proud. To have a boy meant luck was with you.

Grandmama, who believed in the old Chinese religions, often burned incense. "The gods of our ancestors will smell the incense," she said. "They will surely bring us good luck, and a boy."

"Wouldn't it be wonderful if you had a brother?" asked Mother. Li Hua smiled halfheartedly. But the idea only made her jealous.

To celebrate the end of the rice harvest, Mother cooked a special meal. A delicious aroma of ginger and chili sauce filled the house. Li Hua crept up behind Mother in the kitchen and hugged her around the waist.

"Hungry?" asked Mother. Li Hua shook her head glumly.

"Do you want me even if I'm not a boy?"

"Of course. The sun and moon live as a pair," replied Mother, repeating an old Chinese saying. "Brother sun will make sister moon shine. You will be very happy."

But Li Hua could not be made happy. Eating her noodle soup, she daydreamed about what it might have been like, if only she had been a boy.

She remembered again Bobo Lu. Only he had made her feel special, just as she was.

13

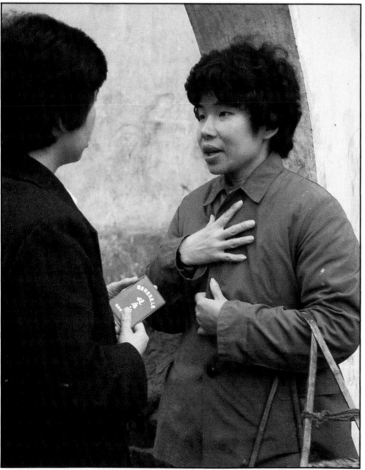

Li Hua's family talked so much about wanting a boy it soon reached the ears of the village cadre. The cadre made sure the people in the village did whatever the government told them to. One day the cadre pulled Li Hua and her mother aside in the street. "Are you planning to have another child?" she asked directly, waving a red book at Mother. Li Hua wondered what her mother had done wrong. "You know how each family is allowed only one child," she added. "It's the official policy."

"Just one more! We need a boy!" pleaded Mother, her hands shaking.

"There are too many people now," said the cadre. "Over one-thousand million living in China. If families have more than one child there will be twice as many people by the time your daughter is as old as you."

From that day on, everyone in Li Hua's family seemed sad. They stopped talking about wanting a boy. And a short time later Mother became sick.

"If I had been a boy none of this would have happened," Li Hua thought. "I've brought bad luck."

Li Hua and Grandmama went on a long walk beside the rice paddies. "Why do only boys bring good luck?" asked Li Hua.

"All children are a blessing," replied Grandmama. "But today, most Chinese families are allowed only one child. So most hope for a strong, healthy boy."

They reached a small town and saw a big billboard showing a happy mother, father, and baby. Above the picture, the slogan read, "One child only, is best for family and nation."

"Why is 'one child only' best?" asked Li Hua.

"When I was a girl," said Grandmama, "families often had ten or more children. To have many children was a blessing. Then China grew too big, too fast. Now people are worried there won't be enough food or land for everyone. One child in a family is all China can feed."

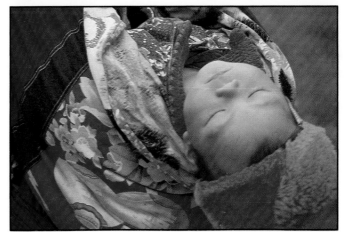

Li Hua's mother became more sick and very pale. She could not get out of bed. Li Hua was told to keep very quiet. The doors and window were kept closed. White strips of cloth were hung outside. Mother was given herbal medicines made from plant roots, leaves, and flowers, which were boiled together.

Grandmama took Li Hua aside. "The potions aren't helping Mother get better," she said in a whisper. "We must do something more."

"What can we do Grandmama?"

"I think we should call on the spirits of all the dead people in our family. Maybe they can help Mother. I've been trying to find out which gods these relatives worshipped. There were so many."

Li Hua suddenly shivered all over. "I feel afraid!" she cried, remembering the funeral she had watched at the market and all the yelling and crying she had seen there. "I don't like to call on the spirits."

"Don't worry," comforted Grandmama. "There was one God your great-uncle talked about. This God loved people and healed them. But it was so long ago, that I cannot remember His name. We'll burn incense in the attic of the house and by the front door. This will keep the bad spirits away."

Li Hua helped Grandmama burn the incense sticks, which filled the house with a strong, musky smell. Grandmama sang some prayers which repeated the names of various Chinese gods. The slow rhythm of the songs was soothing to listen to. Li Hua closed her eyes.

Suddenly Grandmama was quiet. "I know!" she said. "I know of a beautiful old temple, or church, down the river from here. I haven't been there for many years."

Li Hua felt excited. She had been thinking about the forgotten God. "We may find the name of the God who loves and heals people there!"

The next day they travelled downstream in a small boat. The boat carried many other people, animals, and supplies from village to village. The riverbanks were lined with tall bamboo trees and oxen bathed in the water. After passing through the open countryside for several hours, it was time for Grandmama and Li Hua to get off. But when they climbed the riverbank to the temple, Grandmama was shocked by what she saw. There was hardly anything left of the temple. It was just a pile of burned stones.

An old woman appeared at the broken-down entry gate. She told the sad story of what had happened. "The temple was destroyed during the Cultural Revolution. All the monks were driven away or killed."

Grandmama stood with her mouth wide open. "But not all the temples were destroyed, were they?" she asked.

"Nearly all of them," said the woman. "Only a few have been rebuilt since then."

"Come on, Li Hua! **Zou ba**! Let's leave here! This isn't good for you to see!" cried Grandmama, taking Li Hua's hand.

Walking back to where they could catch the boat, Li Hua noticed something carved into a rock. "What's this, Grandmama?"

Grandmama smiled. "It's the Buddha in the middle. He started the Buddhist religion thousands of years ago. The Buddha is worshipped all through China."

"Is that the name of the God my great-uncle believed in?" asked Li Hua.

"No, your great-uncle worshipped a God whom he had said was even greater than the Buddha."

"How can we find out his name?"

"I don't know. It may be impossible," said Grandmama. She squeezed Li Hua's hand and they walked down the slope to the river. The ferryboat had just arrived. Li Hua was very sad that their visit to the temple had been no help at all.

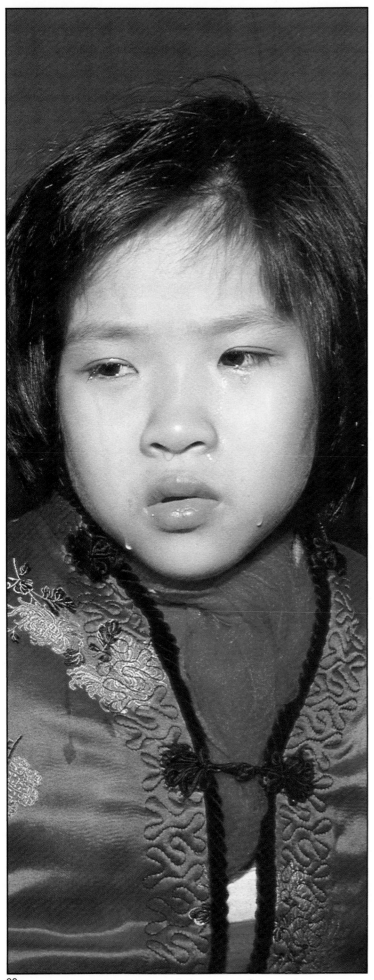

A month went by, and Li Hua's mother still did not get better. Li Hua heard people say Mother might die. She cried herself to sleep almost every night.

One day a neighbor took Li Hua to the market. While she was there, Li Hua remembered how she once had got lost and met Bobo Lu. With him everything had seemed fine. He had even made her feel loved just in the few moments she was with him.

Li Hua wanted to find Bobo Lu. He was not with the men, playing zhi pai. "He's in his new shop," said a man, pointing across the street.

Li Hua asked her neighbor if she could visit a friend. The neighbor said she would meet Li Hua again in an hour. Li Hua hurried across the street jammed with bicycles, and looked up at a freshly painted sign which read "Lu's Clothing."

Inside there was a woman sewing. In the far corner, using an abacus to count money, was Bobo Lu.

"Li Hua! My Beautiful Flower!" he shouted. "What a blessing! Say **ni hao**, hello, to **Ayi**, my wife." In China, children often called older women "Ayi," which meant "Aunty." The couple hugged Li Hua. She began to cry. "What's wrong?" asked Bobo Lu.

"Mama has been very sick for a long time," she sobbed.

"Don't be afraid," said Bobo Lu. "Someone loves your Mama very much. Let me read you a story; then you'll understand what I mean." They sat together on the back step, and Li Hua listened to what she thought was the most wonderful and amazing story she had ever heard. Bobo Lu told her the story came from a book called the Bible. And that the Bible was a book filled with other stories like this one, all true and all about God, whose Son is Jesus.

Later, when Li Hua came home from the market, she was singing a simple song. Grandmama, who was cleaning outside, stopped when she heard the tune. "Li Hua, where did you learn that song?" she asked.

"I learned it today," replied Li Hua.

"I've heard it before!" puzzled Grandmama. "I remember now! Your great-uncle used to sing it ... a long, long time ago ... before he disappeared. Who taught it to you?"

"Bobo Lu."

"Sing the words again ... slowly!" instructed Grandmama.

"Jesus loves me, this I know, for...."

"Jesus! Yes, Jesus!" shouted Grandmama, grabbing Li Hua's hands in joy. "That's His name! He is the One we are looking for!"

Li Hua had not known it at the time, but Bobo Lu had given her the name of the forgotten God, the same one her great-uncle had worshipped.

Grandmama wanted to meet Bobo Lu. It had been so long since she last had seen him, that Grandmama thought he had died. "We'll ask him to come to our home."

The next day Bobo Lu and Ayi visited Li Hua's family. The whole village had heard he was coming, and everyone was very excited. A small group, including the cadre, came to see them. Bobo Lu did not want the attention. He went straight to Mother's room. The others followed and stood at the door, standing on tiptoe to see what was happening.

"I want to pray for your mother," Bobo Lu whispered to Li Hua. "I believe Jesus wants her to get better. We have to ask Him to help Mother. I've seen people healed this way before. It's a very special sign of God's love for us."

He gently laid his hand on Mother's forehead. Nothing very extraordinary seemed to take place. The people watching looked almost disappointed. But Li Hua, who was sitting on the bed holding Mother's hand, felt a wave of warmth tingle right through her. Bobo Lu nodded his head and smiled. "Thank you, Jesus," was all he said. No one heard him except Li Hua.

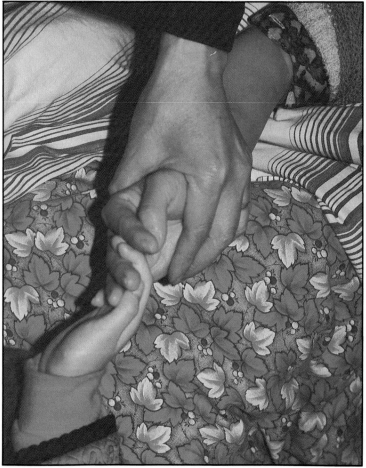

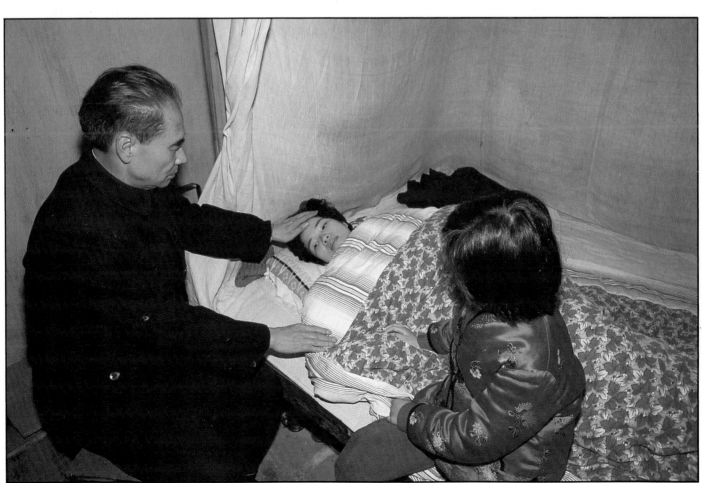

Several days later Mother was up, and soon she was even walking around. The village people were amazed. "Bobo Lu must be a great doctor!" they said to one another.

But Li Hua knew it was Bobo Lu's trusting God and God's love which had healed Mother.

Li Hua and Grandmama opened all the windows and doors. They threw out the pots which held the incense sticks and brought some wild flowers into the house. The pictures of the different Chinese gods which Grandmama had on the walls were taken down, and Li Hua made a little cross out of sticks which she put up in their place. To Li Hua it seemed like all the dark corners were becoming light. She could hardly believe how different everything became. Yet it was not as though things had gone back to the way they were before Mother became sick. Now it was even better. Li Hua could see a change in her whole family.

Mother was very quiet, but always smiling. Grandmama was not complaining so much anymore. And Father was laughing at his old ways, which was something he never used to do.

Father had always been proud of himself that he did not believe in any god. That was what the government taught people to believe.

One day Li Hua overheard Father say, "Deep inside, I knew I was wrong. I cannot live without God. When I did not believe, I thought everything depended on me. If I died and had no son, then my family would struggle. But now I know God cares for my family, and I don't need to be anxious."

Li Hua sighed. Now she knew that Father had wanted what was best for her all along, but had just not been able to show it.

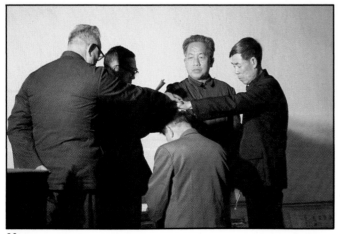

When Bobo Lu visited again, Li Hua had many, many questions. "Are there other people who believe in Jesus?" she asked.

"Many," he said, "but during the Cultural Revolution we had to hide our belief or face death, like your great-uncle. Now we're free to believe again, though the government says there are only certain places where Christians can meet. I know one Church we can visit."

Father was listening and said, "We can all go." Li Hua clapped her hands.

The following Sunday when they arrived at the Church, Li Hua was surprised to see how full it was. Many stood at the back. Everyone looked so excited.

Then they were all quiet when a man stood up at the front. "Today we will celebrate how our Lord Jesus came to give us a new life." His voice was clear and certain.

Li Hua saw Mother wipe away a happy tear. There was so much to be happy about. It didn't matter that Li Hua didn't know all the Chinese characters in the hymn-book, she hummed along as best she could. She joined in the prayers and watched carefully how the leaders prayed for a man by laying their hands on his head, just as Bobo Lu had done. She felt the same love again, but this time it came from all the people.

There was one thing that Li Hua wondered about, though. "Why don't more children come?" she asked an old lady picking up the hymn-books after Church. She had lovely eyes, and Li Hua liked her straight away.

"It's a problem," said the lady. "The government is against children hearing about God because they hope everyone will forget who Jesus is. If we old people are the only ones who remember Him and young ones like you don't hear about Him, then when we die, nobody will know who God is anymore."

"I want to learn more about God," said Li Hua.

The lady stroked Li Hua's hair. "If you love, you will grow," she said. "Nothing can stop love from growing."

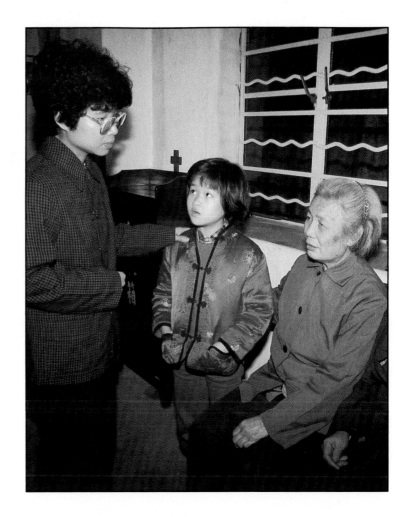

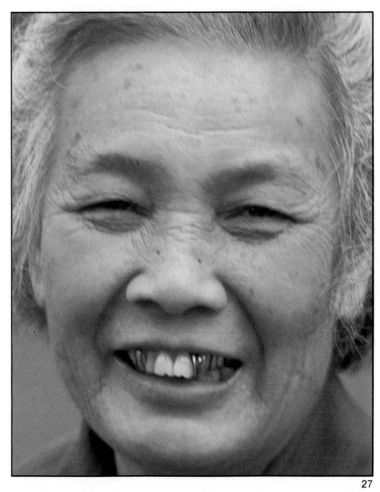

On the way home in the bus Li Hua remembered the lady's words about love. She looked at the hundreds of mountain peaks surrounding her. "God's love must be so big and wide," she thought, "and yet He loves me." She curled up and fell asleep, feeling very much wanted.

When they arrived home, they saw the cadre waiting for them. Li Hua was a little scared by the look on the cadre's face.

"What's this 'Christian Movement'?" asked the cadre. "Some say it has many millions of followers in China. We don't want it here."

"There's no need to be afraid," Mother said bravely to the cadre. "Jesus wants to heal us of our fears, not make new ones. Our country has suffered so much. Now we need to be healed."

Li Hua saw the cadre step back and lower her eyes in agreement.

"Let me show you," added Mother, taking a book from her jacket. Li Hua knew the book. It was a Bible. Bobo Lu had given it to her. Mother told the cadre about one of the stories, about how Jesus had healed a blind man. As Mother explained the story, Li Hua watched from a little way off.

"Now I see what you mean," she heard the cadre say. "Jesus helps us see things in a new way." The cadre's eyes lit up.

Some time after that, Bobo Lu came again to the village. A group gathered around him in a courtyard. Unexpectedly the cadre appeared, and everyone stopped talking and looked worried. Li Hua saw that the cadre no longer looked angry, though. Perhaps the cadre was not as bad as everyone thought.

Mother must have seen the same thing, because she went over and took the cadre by the hand. The group all smiled and relaxed. They welcomed the cadre into their circle. Li Hua knew Jesus was beginning to heal again.

At a meeting a few weeks later Li Hua looked at the different faces in the group of believers from her village. There were smiling faces, peaceful faces, questioning faces, and loving faces. Finally, she stopped at her father's face. He was watching her. Li Hua smiled back, looking deep into his eyes. She remembered again what Father used to be like and how unloved she had felt by him. The memory of that time made her gulp. Then Li Hua saw Father's eyes soften and a huge smile spread across his face. He looked so loving, that Li Hua felt like she wanted to run over and give him a hug right there.

Then Father spoke to the whole group. "We would not be here as believers if it had not been for Li Hua." He called her to him and wrapped his arms around her. "Li Hua, I want to offer you something very special, very rare ... a new name," he said proudly. "This is a name which I had hoped to give to a son. But I now believe this name best describes what you mean to all of us. The name is ... 'Lai Fu.'"

"Lai Fu! Yes, Lai Fu! That's a good name," called out Bobo Lu.

"It means 'Blessing Coming'!" chirped Grandmama with the happiest smile of all.

"God indeed has blessed us through her," said Mother.

Li Hua kissed Father on the cheek. "Thank you for the new name. It is a wonderful name," she said, blushing. "But Jesus loves me just as I am. And because I know He accepts me, I'm happy just as I am, as Li Hua."

"Our Beautiful Flower, loved by God!" exclaimed Father happily, hugging her tightly.